The Littles and the Perfect Christmas

To my mother, Holly Simonds,
whose original idea inspired this story,
and who always made Christmas for us.
And special thanks to Uncle Tom and Aunt Ann.

ISBN 0-439-68703-9

12 11 10 9 8 7 6 5 4 3 2 1 4 5 6 7 8 9/0

Printed in the U.S.A. 40

First printing, December 2004

The Littles and the Perfect Christmas

by **Joel Peterson**
Illustrated by **Jacqueline Rogers**

SCHOLASTIC INC.
New York Toronto London Auckland Sydney
Mexico City New Delhi Hong Kong Buenos Aires

"Callie! Roll over like a good dog," Tom Little shouted.

The Shetland sheepdog looked puzzled. She cocked her head to one side and let out a little whimper. "Roll over! Roll over!" shouted Tom again.

"I don't think it's working," he said to his younger sister, Lucy. "Maybe we need to be closer to her."

Lucy Little looked worried. "I don't know, Tom. You know the rules. We're not supposed to play in wide-open spaces in the house. I don't think Mom and Dad would like it."

"Listen, Lucy," said Tom, "Mrs. Bigg is at Henry's school for a Parents' Day visit

and Mr. Bigg won't be home from work for hours. The house is all ours! There's no way we'll get into trouble. Besides, if Mom and Dad find out, I'll tell them that it was my idea, okay?"

Lucy's face brightened. "Okay, just as long as you're the one who's getting into trouble," she said.

Ten-year-old Tom and eight-year-old Lucy were the two oldest children of Mr. and Mrs. William T. Little. They lived with their parents and their baby sister, Betsy. The children's grandfather and grandmother, and their uncles Pete and Nick lived with them as well.

There wasn't much about them that was very different from any other family. In fact, there were only two things that set them apart from any people that anyone of us might know.

First of all, they were tinies. This meant that they were very, very small.

Mr. Little was the tallest member of

the family. All the rest of his family would tell-you that he stood just six inches high. All of them, that is, except for his wife. Only she knew the truth: Mr. Little was only five and seven-eighths inches tall. He had special inserts in his shoes cut from foam packing material. He claimed that his feet were just more comfortable that way.

The second thing that set tinies apart from bigger people was the fact that they had tails. Their tails were sleek and slim and each one had rich, glossy fur. The tails were just for show; they had no real use. But the Littles were proud of their tails and always kept them well-groomed.

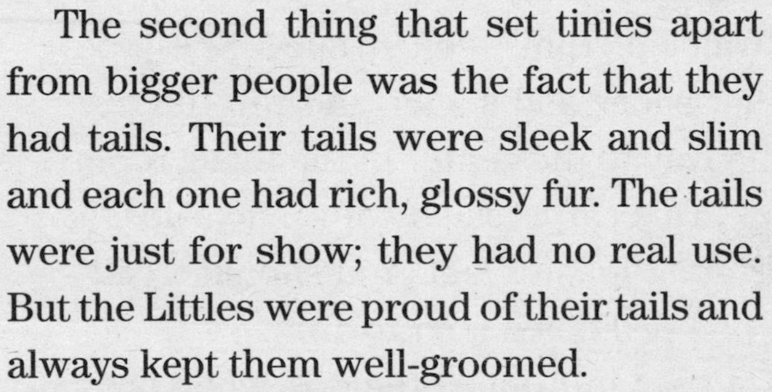

The Little family lived in their own ten-room apartment inside the walls of a house that belonged to a normal-size man named George W. Bigg. Mr. Bigg and his wife and their ten-year-old son, Henry, had no idea that tiny people lived in the house, too.

The Littles would make use of the things the Biggs threw away. In return, the tiny family kept the Biggs' home in good condition. They worked behind the scenes to make sure that the house's plumbing and electricity were trouble-free.

The two tiny children came out from under the sofa where they'd been hiding. Tom walked quickly over to the Biggs' dog. She was stretched out on her side in the middle of the floor.

"Wait up, Tom!" yelled Lucy. She took off her shoes and socks, and ran the rest of the way to the center of the living room floor. "This carpet is so soft," she said. "It feels great in bare feet. You should try it!" She plopped down next to Tom.

They sat in front of the dog while Lucy put her socks and shoes back on.

When Lucy had finished tying her shoes, she and Tom stood up. They walked right over to Callie. The dog rolled from her side onto her belly. She carefully watched the two tiny children. "Well, she rolled *up*, at least," said Lucy. "Maybe next time she'll roll *over.*"

The two children stood right in front of Callie's shiny black nose.

"Roll over," said Tom again. "Come on, roll over."

Only Callie didn't roll over. She was too relaxed to do anything. All of a sudden, her huge mouth opened as wide as it could open, right in front of the children's eyes. They could see every one of her teeth, as well as her long, wet, pink tongue. In fact, they could just about see her tonsils.

"Oh, man, she's yawning! That is so cool!" said Tom. "I've never seen anything like that!"

"Well, I've never smelled anything like that," said his sister, holding her nose. "Dog breath stinks! Yuck!"

Suddenly, they heard a key jiggling in the front door lock. "Oh, no!" said Lucy.

The two tiny children were out in the middle of the living room floor. The closest piece of furniture they could hide behind was several feet away.

Tom grabbed Lucy's hand. "Come on!"

he whispered. "Hurry!" They ran around Callie, and pushed themselves into her warm, furry side.

The front door opened, and Mr. Bigg came walking into the living room. A burst of cold December air blew in from outside.

"What's he doing home now?" Lucy whispered to Tom. "He's not supposed to be home this early!"

Mr. Bigg walked over to Callie. "Does somebody want to go bye-bye?" he asked in a baby-talk voice. The children heard Callie's license tags jingle as her head whipped around toward Mr. Bigg.

"Hang on, Lucy!" said Tom.

"Huh?" asked Lucy, staring at her brother.

"Hang on! Like this," said Tom. He grabbed hold of the long black-and-white hair on the dog's belly. Lucy did the same.

"Bye-bye?" asked Mr. Bigg again.

Callie stood up very quickly. Tom and Lucy held on for dear life as Callie ran toward the front door.

The dog leapt through the doorway. She cleared the front steps, landed in the front yard, and began running around in circles.

The front door of the house closed. The dog stopped for a second. Tom and Lucy were still holding tightly onto her belly fur. They could barely see each other through the long, silky strands.

"How are you doing, Lucy?" Tom asked his sister.

"My arms are getting tired," she panted. "I'm a little dizzy, too."

"Hang on tight!" yelled Tom. "Here we go again!"

The dog raced like lightning around the side of the house toward the backyard. Tom Little looked down. The ground was whizzing by underneath them.

"Lucy!" he yelled back to his sister. "Whatever you do, don't look down!"

"Too late!" Lucy yelled back. When the dog got to the backyard, she continued to run around in circles.

Mr. Bigg stood in the back door. "Come on, Cal," he said. "Do your business, or come in."

"Business?" asked Lucy. "Is he nuts? What kind of business does a dog do?"

"Don't ask," said Tom. "Just hold on."

"Callie!" yelled Mr. Bigg. "Get in here, and quit wasting my time." The dog raced back toward the house.

Callie ran right past Mr. Bigg, and stopped in the living room. She ended up right where the whole crazy ride had begun.

Mr. Bigg was still closing the back door. There were two rooms between him and the two tiny children. Tom and Lucy let go of the dog's fur and tumbled onto the living room carpet. They ran as fast as they could toward the sofa. Just as Mr. Bigg came back into the room, they dove underneath.

"Lucy!" said Tom, out of breath. "Are you all right?"

"I'm okay," she said. Tom couldn't see her, but he thought he could hear a smile in his sister's voice. "Let's do it again!" she said. "That was fun!"

"So, did you two do anything interesting today?" Mrs. Little asked Tom. It was six o'clock in the evening. The Little family had just settled down to eat dinner. On the other side of the wall, the Biggs were just sitting down to their own supper.

The Littles usually ate whatever the Biggs were having, and this evening was no exception. Tonight, everyone in the house was enjoying leftover Chinese food.

"Oh, you know, Mom," said Tom, "we didn't do anything special. We ended up just hanging around the house."

"Yeah," Lucy piped up, "we were just hanging around and around and around and around..."

"Mr. Bigg came home early," said Tom, quickly changing the subject.

"He did?" said Mr. Little. "That's funny. It's not a holiday or anything. I wonder if everything's okay."

"Well, there's one way to find out," said Uncle Pete. He got up and walked over to the dining room wall.

Uncle Pete used a cane and walked with a slight limp. He had been injured during the Great Mouse Invasion of the last century.

Uncle Pete turned toward the table of tiny people, and put his finger to his lips. When everyone was silent, he turned back to the wall. He put both hands on either side of a large cork that was stuck in a hole in the wall, just above the Littles' sofa. He carefully pulled it out.

Inside of the hole where the cork had been was a thin layer of wallpaper that was full of pinholes. Just on the other side sat the members of the Bigg family.

Most of the time, the Littles tried not

to listen in on the Biggs. Dinnertime was another matter entirely. This was the time when the Littles got most of their news from the outside world as Mr. and Mrs. Bigg talked about current events.

Tonight was different somehow. The Biggs weren't laughing and joking around as they usually did during meals.

The Littles listened very quietly as they ate their dinner. The Biggs had just finished eating.

"I think Callie needs to go out," said Mr. Bigg to his son. "Why don't you take her for a quick walk?"

"That's a good idea," said Mrs. Bigg. "Be sure to wear your winter coat, Henry. This December feels more like the middle of January, if you ask me."

Henry bundled up to go outside. The Sheltie barked and wagged her tail as Henry put on her leash and led her out the door. Both his parents waited until they heard the front door close before they continued talking.

Mr. Bigg was the first to speak. "Fifteen years. Fifteen long years I worked for the Big Valley Phone Company, and this is how they treat me. 'We need to run a leaner

company,' they said. Do you know that last week they removed the water coolers from the office, just to save a buck? The water coolers, for crying out loud! Like supplying their workers with water during the day is going to bankrupt them!"

"It's not fair, George," his wife said.

"You're darn right it's not fair!" said Mr. Bigg. He sounded angry, and his voice was getting louder. "Do you know what they told me? They said they needed to downsize the company. They're downsizing me, that's what they're doing!"

Mr. Bigg shook his head. "I don't know what we're going to do for money," he said. "I don't know how we're going to put food on the table. I don't know," he said, almost under his breath, "how we're going to manage to keep our house."

"You mustn't talk like that, George!" said Mrs. Bigg. "We're going to be just fine. I was a dental assistant before we got married, remember? I'm sure I can find a job. When I was working, Dr. Flossumgoode said that

I was the best helper that he'd ever had."

"I suppose I could work somewhere, too," said Mr. Bigg. "Maybe Vast Mart needs some part-time workers. After all, Christmas is only a few weeks away."

"No," said Mrs. Bigg. "No, I don't think you should do that. We've got some money saved up. For the next few weeks, I think you should relax, and do what you love to do." Mrs. Bigg stood up and started to clear dishes from the table.

"You should work on some projects downstairs in your workshop," she suggested. "Finish building the Christmas present that you're making for Henry. You need to clear your head. I don't think rushing right into a part-time job is the way to do that."

"Maybe you're right," said Mr. Bigg. He sounded a little less upset. "I really do need to clear my head, just forget the Big Valley Phone Company."

His voice began to get very loud again. "I don't want to waste time even thinking about those no-good, dirty, low-down..."

Uncle Pete quickly stuffed the cork back into the dining room wall. He limped back to the dinner table.

"I don't like the sound of this," he said. "Poor Mr. Bigg. To have the rug yanked out from underneath him like this. It just doesn't seem fair."

"And during the holidays, too," said Mrs. Little. "The people that run that company are a bunch of Scrooges. There must be something we can do to help out."

Lucy had a puzzled look on her face. "Mother, is Mr. Bigg going to become one of us tinies?" she asked.

"Heavens, no, Lucy," she said. "Why on earth would you think such a thing?"

"He said he was going to be downsized," said the tiny girl with a frown.

"Oh, brother!" moaned Tom. He put his elbows on the table and covered his eyes with his hands.

"Tom!" said his father. "Stop making fun of your sister and get your elbows off of the table!"

Tom quickly sat up straight.

"Now," said Mr. Little, "make yourself useful, and go get the dessert."

Tom ran to the Littles' kitchen, and came back with a fortune cookie. It was so big he had to carry it in both hands. He put it on the floor, and popped the cellophane wrapper by stomping on one end. Then he lifted the fortune cookie up onto the table.

"Lucy," said Mr. Little, "would you care to do the honors?" Lucy nodded eagerly.

Mr. Little handed the girl a metal door key. They kept the old key hanging on the wall. Sometimes they used it to crack open peanut shells.

Lucy held the narrow end of the key, and raised the other end over her head like an axe. She swung it down right into the

center of the cookie. It broke into small pieces.

Her family clapped and laughed as they took pieces of the cookie.

"Good job! Read us the fortune, Lucy!" said Grandpa Little.

"Yes, read us the fortune!" everyone cried out at once. Lucy picked up the strip of paper from the broken bits of cookie. She held it out in front of her, and spread both arms wide in order to read what was printed on the paper.

"'The past is behind you,'" Lucy read slowly. "'The key to the future lies in the present.'"

Tom and Lucy Little sat on top of a hot water pipe in the Biggs' root cellar. From the place they were sitting, they could look through a hole in the basement wall into the room next door.

The room was their favorite room in the whole house. It was Mr. Bigg's workshop. Mr. Bigg wasn't in his workshop at the moment, but the light was on, and the children could clearly see everything in the room.

"Do you think that's the present that the fortune was talking about, Tom?" asked Lucy. She was pointing to a large green-and-white striped tent that hung down from the ceiling and covered most of Mr. Bigg's workbench.

Tom Little laughed. "It wasn't that kind of present, dodo. It meant *the* present.

You know, like the here-and-now kind of present—not a gift."

Lucy looked hurt. "I'm not a dodo. I think it meant a real present." She pointed through the hole. "Mr. Bigg's secret Christmas present for Henry."

"Think about it, Lucy," said Tom. "The fortune said that the key to the future is in the present. I suppose you think there's a real key in there, also?"

"Well," said Lucy, "I did use a real key to open the cookie. I just think the fortune was about a Christmas present, that's all."

"I think you're both right," said a voice behind them. Tom and Lucy froze in terror. They turned around. It was just their father.

"In fact," Mr. Little said, "I'm present right at this moment to talk to you about a present—a Christmas present for your mother. I've spoken to all the other family members about this except for the two of you. Since your mother never comes down here, this is the perfect place to tell you!" said Mr. Little. He sat down on the pipe.

"You know that every Christmas we draw names out of a bottle cap?"

"Sure," said Tom. "Then we make or find a gift for the person whose name we draw."

"Right," said their dad. "Well, we'll do that again this year, but there's also something extra that I think we should do for Mom. I don't know if you two know this, but some people get sort of sad around the holiday season."

"That shouldn't be," said Lucy. "It's the happiest time of year!"

"Not for everyone, Lucy," her father said. "Some people feel down in the dumps during this time of year, and your mother is one of them. She tries very hard to make Christmas special for everyone else, and she does a wonderful job. That's why we want to make this Christmas the best ever for your mother. But you have to promise not to say anything to her about it. It's a surprise."

"You can trust us, Dad," said Tom. "We're good secret keepers."

Lucy nodded her head.

"Good deal," said their father. "Let's pinky-swear on it."

Tom and Lucy held out their pinkies. Mr. Little held out both his hands, and curled both his pinkies around the children's. Lucy giggled as the three of them shook their hands up and down.

"Speaking of secrets," said Mr. Little, "what's underneath that big tent thing?" He pointed at the green-and-white tent covering Mr. Bigg's workbench.

"All we know is that it's some kind of a Christmas present for Henry," said Tom. "Mr. Bigg mostly works on it at night. By the time he starts working on it, we're in bed."

"Well," said Mr. Little, "now that Mr. Bigg has lost his job, I'm sure he'll be down here a lot more during the daytime. There's a good chance you're going to find out what Henry's present is before too long."

He held up his pinkies again. Tom and Lucy held up theirs. "Now before I tell you about your mother's special Christmas present, remember, mum's the word!" Tom, Lucy, and Mr. Little shook pinkies one more time.

"Okay," Mr. Little said, "listen closely. This is what we're going to do...."

The very next afternoon, Tom and Lucy were back in their hiding place in the Biggs' root cellar. They were watching Mr. Bigg. He was putting the final touches on a small wooden tiger cub figurine. The Biggs' real cat, Hildy, sat on a stool watching.

As Mr. Bigg lightly sanded the piece, he spoke to it as if it were alive.

"There you go, Stripy. Almost finished. You're a good-looking cat, you know that?" Mr. Bigg began to turn the tiger around in his hands, making sure that it was perfect.

Then he showed it to Hildy. "What do you think of your little cousin, Hildy?"

Lucy giggled as Hildy touched noses with the tiny tiger cub.

Hildy was the Littles' friend. Tom had

tamed her long ago—long before Callie came to live in the house.

"George!" Mrs. Bigg called from the top of the cellar stairs. "You'd better hurry! The matinee at the Bargain Cinema starts in half an hour, and we don't want to be late."

"Okay, honey," Mr. Bigg called out. "By the way, I think this is a great idea. A cheap Saturday afternoon at the movies will be just the thing to take our minds off our troubles. What are we going to see?"

"It's a foreign film," she yelled down. "You know, the kind with subtitles."

"Oh?" said Mr. Bigg, raising his eyebrows while sanding the tiger cub.

"Yes—Henry picked it out," she yelled. "It's called *Octopon Versus the Squid Women from Atlantis*. I think it's Japanese."

"Oh," said Mr. Bigg. He rolled his eyes. "Okay, I'll be right there."

He gave the little tiger one last swipe with the sandpaper. "All done, pal. Time for you to join your little friends."

Mr. Bigg grabbed the end of a rope that was dangling next to his workbench. The rope ran through a pulley near the basement ceiling. The other end was attached to the top of the green-and-white striped tent on the workbench. He gave a sharp tug on the rope, and the tent rose quickly up to the ceiling.

Tom and Lucy each let out a sharp gasp. There below them, spread out over half of Mr. Bigg's workbench, was a perfect, tiny, three-ring circus. The tiny children couldn't believe their eyes! It was as though it was custom-made especially for someone who was just their size.

"George!" yelled Mrs. Bigg again.

"All right, all right! I'll be right there," Mr. Bigg called. He placed the tiny tiger in the center ring of the circus.

"Time to go, Hildy," he said. He picked up the cat and walked quickly up the basement stairs. He was in such a hurry, he forgot to turn off the workbench light and to cover Henry's present.

Tom and Lucy didn't move a muscle until they heard the front door shut. They remained still and stared at the circus until they heard the doors of the Biggs' car slam, and the car drive away.

Tom was the first to break the silence. He looked at his sister. A huge grin spread across his face. "I'll race you!" he shouted. "Come on!"

Lucy and Tom squeezed through a tiny space in the wall above the water pipe. They ran along the top of the pipe. Finally, they were just above the workbench. The green-and-white tent hung just above their heads.

As they looked down, they could see Mr. Bigg's amazing circus spread out below them. Three large wooden rings were built in the middle of the circus. Each ring was about a foot wide and two inches high with an opening cut into the side.

The rings rested on top of a piece of plywood. Most of the plywood was painted dark blue. Brightly painted paths of red and green squares ran looping through and around the three rings. Here and there, yellow stars stood out on the blue surface.

There were three towers with ladders, one in each of the rings. The one in the middle looked like a high-diving platform. A long, tight, steel wire connected the towers that stood in the two side rings.

Inside the rings and all around were beautiful wooden figurines of clowns and other circus performers. There were lion tamers, trapeze artists, and one colorful figure in a top hat that looked like the ring-master.

Wooden bears, ponies, lions, and tigers were also spread out around the floor of the circus. There was even a big, beautiful elephant figurine with long wooden tusks.

Some of the figures had been painted and varnished. Some were still unfinished wood. Mr. Bigg hadn't painted them yet.

The children could see a wooden box at one end of the circus. They also noticed two painted panels that stood about a foot high on either end of the circus. From where they stood on the pipe, they couldn't tell exactly what was painted on the panels.

"How do we get down?" Lucy asked. She was so excited that she was shaking a little bit.

Tom looked around for a minute. "There!" he said. He was pointing to a cabinet at the back of the workbench. Many of the cabinet drawers were half-open. They were filled with all sorts of nails, screws, brackets, and other small things that Mr. Bigg used when working with wood.

Because so many of the drawers were open, Tom and Lucy had no trouble climbing down the cabinet like a pair of tiny rock climbers.

Tom and Lucy jumped onto the workbench and walked across the top. It was littered with all sorts of painting materials—tubes of paint, paintbrushes, and jars of murky colored water that he used to clean them. There were lots of sponges and pieces of sandpaper.

The whole surface was covered with newspaper. It was there in case Mr. Bigg made a mess while he was painting.

Mrs. Bigg had made her husband leave for the movies so quickly that afternoon, he had even left some of his lunch behind: a half-eaten baloney sandwich, some potato chips, and a can of cola with a straw in it.

Tom helped himself to a chip as he walked past Mr. Bigg's lunch plate. He held it with both hands, loudly chomping pieces out of it.

"Tom," scolded his sister, "you know Mom and Dad don't like us to eat junk food!"

Tom shrugged. "They won't find out. Besides, I've heard that when people go to the circus, they're supposed to eat stuff that's bad for them."

"Still," said Lucy, "I don't think it's a good idea to—" Tom looked at his sister. She was staring straight ahead.

"Oh, Tom—" she began. "Oh, Tom! It's totally awesome!" The two of them stepped onto the plywood floor of Mr. Bigg's circus. From there, they could clearly see what was painted on the two panels that stood a foot tall on either side of them.

The one Lucy was looking at showed about a hundred people. Some were clapping, some were cheering, and some were munching on popcorn.

"Whoa!" said Tom. "You can almost hear the roar of the crowd!" He walked along, looking at the painted wall. "Their eyes seem to look at you no matter where you stand. This must be what rock stars feel like on stage!"

Lucy was already running across the floor of the circus to the other side. She stood in front of the opposite panel. The word "Midway" was written across the top of the wall, in tiny lights of all colors.

Lucy ran around behind the panel, and saw an electrical plug. She plugged it into a nearby outlet, and ran back around and into the circus. The Midway

sign was flashing one letter after another, followed by all of the letters at once.

"Tom!" Lucy yelled. Her brother ran over, zigzagging through the wooden circus figures that were scattered across the circus floor.

"Oh, man!" said her brother. "This place just keeps getting better and better!"

The children walked along the Midway. There were painted booths featuring all sorts of strange and wonderful sideshow

folks. There was an old-lady fortune-teller and a rubber man who had tied his arms and legs into a human knot. There was a beautiful half-woman, half-fish mermaid and a man with an old-fashioned mustache who was swallowing an entire sword!

Tom and Lucy laughed as they pointed at all the different characters. Their favorite was Kluck-Kluck the Amazing Chicken Man. He looked like a man, but he had chicken wings for arms and drumsticks for legs. He was covered in feathers and had a bird beak for a nose.

"Look!" cried Lucy. She ran up to a big spinning wheel that was sticking out from the Midway panel. Above it were painted the words: "Wheel of Chance! Try Your Luck!" Words were printed on squares all around the outside of the wheel.

"Give it a whirl! See what it lands on!" said Tom.

Lucy reached up over her head, and grabbed the wheel with both hands. She pulled down as hard as she could. There was a very loud and fast clicking noise as the wheel flew around. As it slowed down, so did the clicking. Finally, an arrow on the wheel pointed to the words "Go Directly to the Center Ring!"

Lucy quickly ran to the center ring. Tom continued eating his potato chip as he walked along looking at the strange and wonderful sights along the Midway.

Lucy gasped as she walked through the open doorway on the side of the center ring. There, next to the tiger cub Mr. Bigg had been working on a few minutes before, was a bigger, beautiful, wooden tiger. It stood on its hind legs, right in front of Lucy. Mr. Bigg had carefully painted the ferocious creature himself. It looked very real to the tiny girl.

Lucy lifted her head and looked up at the high-diving platform above her head. She could see the shiny high wire cutting through the air. It was even higher than the diving platform. It stretched between the two poles in the side rings. It was the tallest point in the whole circus. It was at least a foot and a half above her head.

"Awesome," she whispered to herself. She walked over to a small wooden box, and opened it up. Inside were some cards, some yellow, star-shaped pieces of painted wood, and a pair of dice.

There was also a rolled-up piece of paper with a list of some sort, in Mr. Bigg's handwriting.

Lucy carefully unrolled the paper. She got down on her knees and began to read. "Tom!" she called out. "It's not just a circus. It's a game! A whole neat game with rules that Mr. Bigg made up!"

Tom didn't answer her. Lucy walked along one of the paths in the ring, carefully stepping on the red and green squares. She stopped and scratched her head as she looked down. According to the instructions, she should be on a green square, but the one she was standing on was bright red. Lucy shrugged her shoulders and looked around. Tom was nowhere to be found.

She yelled even louder. “Tom! It’s a game! Let’s play! Where are you?” Still, there was no response. Lucy took a deep breath and shouted at the top of her lungs: “Tom Little! Where are you?”

It was then that she heard his voice, from way up high above her head. “Up here, Luce. Here I am!”

Lucy looked up. Her mouth opened to scream, but no sound came out.

There, what seemed like a mile above her head, her big brother was inching his way across the high wire. He was carefully putting one foot in front of the other, and looking straight ahead. He held Mr. Bigg's drinking straw in both hands for balance. The straw stuck out four inches on either side of his body.

Lucy held her hands over her mouth. She knew that if she screamed, her brother might fall, and there wasn't any safety net to catch him. Somehow, she managed to calm herself down.

"Tom?" Lucy spoke very calmly. "That's not a good idea. There isn't a net."

"No problem," said Tom. He was staring

straight ahead at the platform at the other end of the wire. "I'm The Great Tom Little! I always work without a net. I dazzled the crowned heads of Europe with my daring feats of daredeviltry!"

"Tom, please come down," said Lucy. "I'm scared you're going to fall!"

"I'm not going to fall," Tom said. He sounded annoyed. "Besides, I'm halfway across. I can't turn back now."

Lucy thought quickly. She looked around. She noticed that some of the things that Mr. Bigg had been using to paint the circus were still scattered about the surface of the game.

Right next to her in the center ring she saw an old sardine can filled with green acrylic paint and a large, soft sponge.

Lucy put both hands at the end of the sponge and began to push it along underneath Tom.

"Lucy, what are you doing?" Tom asked without looking down.

"What do you think I'm doing?" she asked. "I'm making sure you don't break your neck when you fall."

"Darn it, Lucy! I told you I can do this. I don't need your help."

Tom looked down at his sister. All the color drained from his face. He lost his concentration and his balance at the same time. He began to teeter back and forth on the wire.

Lucy screamed as Tom dropped the straw and fell from the wire. She gave the sponge one last shove.

Tom's arms and legs waved around like crazy as he dropped through the air. He landed right in the middle of the sponge.

"Tom!" Lucy cried. "Oh, my gosh! Are you okay?"

Slowly, Tom peeled himself off the sponge. The sponge was still damp with some watery green paint. Tom's face, hands, and the front of his clothes were a pale mint-green color.

Now that she could see Tom was still in one piece, Lucy realized how ridiculous he looked. She couldn't help laughing.

"What's so funny?" Tom asked. He sounded angry.

"You are," his sister said, pointing at him. "You look just like the Jolly Green Elf."

Tom looked at his hands. He couldn't help laughing himself.

"Let's go," he said. "I need to take a bath."

Lucy pushed the sponge back to where it was when she found it, and Tom put the straw back in the cola can. The tiny family didn't know what would happen if the Biggs found out about them—so they were very careful to leave things just as they had found them.

The two tiny children walked back to the cabinet. They stopped to take one last look at the wonderful Midway. The lights on the sign were still blinking.

"Uh-oh," Lucy said. "Be right back." She ran across the table and behind the circus.

Tom watched as the lights went out. Lucy came out from behind the circus wall. She was walking back to meet Tom, when she stopped in her tracks.

She walked backward on the newspaper that covered the worktable. A small newspaper advertisement had caught her eye. *Are You a Craftsperson?* the ad read. *Do You Make Toys? Sign Up Now for the Big Valley Christmas Craft Fair!*

"Tom!" Lucy shouted, as she picked up a red marking pen from the tabletop. Her brother ran over and joined her.

"What's up?" he asked.

"Help me out for a minute, will you?" Lucy asked. She pointed the pen at Tom. "When I say 'now,' pull the cap off." She braced herself as Tom firmly gripped the cap of the marking pen.

"Now!" yelled Lucy. The cap slid off as Tom pulled. Somehow he managed to get red from the tip of the marker on his hands as he stumbled backward. He looked down at his red-and-green fingers.

"It's just not my day," he sighed.

Lucy and Tom used the marker to circle the ad in the paper.

"I hope Mr. Bigg sees this ad in time to enter the craft fair," said Lucy.

She and Tom carefully placed the cap back on the marker and headed for home.

Tom and Lucy stood in the passageway that led to the front door of their family's apartment.

"Listen, Lucy," said Tom, "just pretend nothing's wrong, okay? Maybe that way we can sneak past them."

Lucy gulped and nodded. Tom turned the knob and opened the door.

His mother, father, grandparents, and both of his uncles were sitting in the living room. They all looked up and stared at Tom and Lucy. Uncle Nick's pipe fell out of his mouth. Uncle Pete let out a whistle. "Great Tiny in the Sky!" he exclaimed. "What in the world happened to you, Tom?"

Before Tom had a chance to say anything, Lucy jumped in and told the whole story.

As she talked, she waved her arms wildly about, describing the wonderful circus that they had found. She didn't leave out any details, especially when it came time to tell about her brother's big-top adventure. She was especially proud of the part where she'd pushed the sponge underneath Tom and saved his life.

When she finished, she was out of breath from talking so fast.

Tom just stared at his sister. "Did you have to tell them *everything*?" he said.

"Tom!" scolded his mother. "Lucy was right to tell us all about what happened. You could have been hurt very badly if you'd fallen on the hard table."

"That's right, Tom," Granny Little said. She had a very stern look on her face. "You should be thankful for what your sister did."

Mr. Little turned and faced the family.

"Have you ever heard of any young tiny who was so reckless?"

"Well," said Uncle Nick as he stood up,

"Dinky's pretty reckless when he flies around in that glider of his."

"Dinky wears a seat belt and a parachute, Nick," replied Mr. Little. "And despite the fact that he doesn't act like one, he actually is an adult, remember?"

"Oh, yeah, I guess he is sort of a grown-up," Uncle Nick said quietly. He sat down.

Tom went off to wash up. The rest of the family was very curious to hear more about Tom and Lucy's discovery. Lucy did her best to describe in detail everything she had seen, including the rules for playing the game.

"What a lovely gift for Henry!" said her mother. "It sounds just perfect!"

Lucy thought for a moment, and frowned. "It's almost perfect," she said. "I just remembered something that I think may be wrong."

Lucy pictured the circus in her mind. "Mr. Bigg painted paths all over the board that you're supposed to follow when you play the game. The paths are made of red and green squares. You know, a red square, then a green square, red, green, like that. But in one place, there are two red ones in a row. That means all the rest of them are the wrong color. The red ones should be green and the green ones should be red."

"Oh, my," said Mrs. Little. "He must have made a mistake. That will ruin the whole game, won't it?"

"Not if we fix it!" said Lucy.

"I don't see that we have time, Lucy," said her father. "Even if we all pitched in and helped, Mr. Bigg would have to be out of the house long enough for us to do the work."

"So?" said Lucy.

"So," her father said, "Christmas is only two days away. I'm sure Mr. Bigg will be spending Christmas Eve with his family."

"I'll bet he spends the whole day out of the house tomorrow," said Lucy.

Just then Tom walked into the living room. He was back to his old color. "I'll bet he doesn't," he said.

"Hands up, who agrees with me?" asked Lucy. Nobody raised a hand.

"Hands up, who agrees with Tom?" Everyone's hand shot up. Lucy saw that Tom still had a bit of red on his hand.

"All right," she said with a sly smile, "hands up, who wants to help fix Henry's circus if Mr. Bigg *does* spend the whole day away from the house tomorrow?"

Everybody raised their hands—except Granny.

"I'm not going down to that basement," she said. "Not for anything."

"Don't worry. It'll never happen," Uncle Nick whispered to Uncle Pete. "Everybody stays home on Christmas Eve. The poor man doesn't even have a job. He's not going anywhere tomorrow."

"Okay, Lucy," said her mother. "You win that one. If Mr. Bigg spends Christmas Eve out of the house, we'll spend a few hours in the basement fixing the game." She stood up.

"Speaking of Christmas, I think I need to spend a little more time on your presents today. I never feel as though I've done enough for everyone during the holidays."

Lucy hugged her mother. "You make Christmas great!" she said. "And this year, we're going to make your Christmas great, too!"

Lucy saw her father hold his finger to his lips as a signal for her to keep quiet about the secret present.

Lucy winked at her dad. She closed her eyes and hugged her mother a little harder.

The next morning, Lucy Little walked into her family's living room. Her two uncles were sitting on the sofa. They were reading a tiny newspaper. Lucy had never seen it before.

"What's that?" she asked. Her family usually got their news from whatever radio or television station the Biggs happened to be listening to or watching.

"It's called the Trash City *Tabloid*," said Uncle Nick. "Your Cousin Dinky dropped it off the last time he delivered the mail. It's a brand-new newspaper that's published out of Trash City. It covers all the tiny news in the Big Valley. This issue's a little out of date, but I haven't read it yet, so it's all news to me."

"Humph!" scoffed Uncle Pete. "This paper's nothing but a sleazy scandal sheet. Anyone could tell just by the headline: 'Mutant Baffles Scientists: Tiny born without a tail.'" He threw his section of the paper on the sofa.

"As far as I'm concerned," he said, "there's only one paper worth reading: the *Tiny Times Gazette*. It's published by the Library Tinies, and everything in it is one hundred percent fact."

Lucy stood up on the sofa between her two uncles. "I guess we'll have to get the news the old-fashioned way," she said.

She carefully removed the cork from the wall. The three tinies were very quiet. They could hear the television news in the background. Suddenly, they heard Mr. Bigg speaking to someone. They could only hear Mr. Bigg, and not the other person.

"He must be on the phone," whispered Lucy.

“That sounds great, Charlie,” Mr. Bigg was saying. “So it’s not too late? I can set up a table at the craft fair today?”

He paused before speaking again. “Well, that’s just wonderful. I thought that all the places would be taken.” Mr. Bigg stopped talking again. He was listening to the person on the other end of the phone.

After a while, he spoke up again. “I agree, Charlie. It is a great opportunity to sell some of my toys and make some money. That’s right: What’s Christmas without toys? No, I don’t think my wife will be too upset with me being at the crafts fair on Christmas Eve. After all, she must have wanted me to go. Who else would have marked the ad in the paper for me—some little green elf? Ha! Ha!”

He paused, then spoke again. “Good talking to you, too. I’ll be there in about an

hour or so to register. I just have to pack my stuff into the car. Talk to you soon, Charlie. Bye." Mr. Bigg hung up the phone.

Lucy stuffed the cork back into the wall. She jumped off of the couch. She rubbed her hands together matter-of-factly.

"It's a go!" Lucy said to her uncles. "It should only take a couple hours to fix the game if we all pitch in. Wear old clothes that you don't mind getting paint on. I'll go and tell everyone else." She ran off.

Uncle Nick looked at Uncle Pete. "How could she have known?" he asked. Uncle Pete sighed and shrugged his shoulders. "Beats me," he said. "Maybe she's psychic."

Uncle Nick looked disgusted. "Maybe she's psychic!" he mimicked. "Phooey!"

"See?" said Lucy Little. "There are two red squares in a row. That throws off the whole game. From that point until the end, all the red ones should be green, and all the green ones should be red!"

She was standing in the center ring of the circus. Her family stood around her, taking in Mr. Bigg's amazing creation.

"Outstanding!" Grandpa Little kept saying as he walked through the circus. Every so often, he'd lift his glasses off of his nose and stare right into the delicately carved face of a wooden bear, or tiger, or circus performer.

"Really quite extraordinary!" he'd say, as he looked over every detail.

"Lucy's right," said Mr. Little. "We'll need to work fast. Lucy, you're sure that the path on the game board isn't painted correctly? You read through all of the rules?"

The little girl nodded her head.

"Okay," said her father, looking around, "it looks like Mr. Bigg certainly has enough paint mixed up for the job. Let's see if we can find some paintbrushes or some sort of tools to work with."

"We're ahead of you on that one, Dad," Tom said.

He walked over to a paint rag that was lying next to Mr. Bigg's painting materials. Tom grabbed one end of the rag with both hands and gave it a sharp tug. The Littles gathered around to see what was underneath.

"Well, look at that," Uncle Nick said. "The boy has thought of everything!"

He was looking at a pile of tiny paint rollers that Tom and Lucy had made themselves. They had cleverly bent pieces of paper clips into L-shapes, and placed tube-shaped foam packing material on the ends of each one. They had also made paint trays for everyone out of heavy-duty tin-foil. Tom handed rollers to his parents and his uncles.

"The idea," said Tom, "is that five of us, me included, take turns leapfrogging in front of each other, and just change the colors as quickly as we can."

He handed his grandfather a pair of fine paintbrushes. "Grandpa has the steadiest hands," said Tom. The whole family chuckled, because it was true. Grandpa Little was the oldest member of the family, but when it came to doing fine work, he was the best.

"Grandpa, you follow behind us and paint the edges of the green and red squares. I've given you a brush for each color. Uncle Pete will hold whichever brush you're not using at the moment. He'll also keep moving these two bottle caps full of paint along the line, so that you don't have to worry about them."

Grandpa looked down at the bottle caps of red and green paint. He grinned. "Yes, sir!" he said to Tom, as he saluted his grandson. He looked at the rest of the family and winked.

"We'd better get rolling," said Lucy. "Mr. Bigg is at the craft fair, but we have no idea when Mrs. Bigg and Henry will be back from their Christmas shopping."

"More like window shopping, unfortunately," said Mrs. Little. "Even with Mrs. Bigg working at that dentist's office, I know that their savings are dwindling, and Christmas will be very hard to manage this year. I heard them talking the other day."

"Well," said Uncle Pete, "at least Henry will have this stupendous circus that his father built for him. I'd say that Mr. Bigg is a lot like Grandpa—still a kid at heart."

"It's lucky for the rest of you that some of us never get old," said Grandpa. "We're the dreamers and inventors. Where would you be without us?"

"I can't imagine," said Lucy. And she gave her grandpa a big hug.

When the last green square had a new coat of red paint, and Grandpa Little had carefully given it a nice straight edge, everyone put down their tools. They looked back at the neatly repainted path.

"It looks really good, if I say so myself," said Uncle Pete.

“It sure does,” said Lucy. “I knew that if we all worked hard together, it wouldn’t take much time at all.”

Just then, the Littles heard the front door of the house slam shut. “Great Gooey Gopher Guts!” whispered Uncle Pete. “Someone’s home early!”

“It’s probably just Henry and Mrs. Bigg,” said Mrs. Little. “Henry’s not allowed to come down here so he doesn’t spoil his Christmas surprise, and Mrs. Bigg usually only comes down on laundry day.”

Everyone breathed a sigh of relief. Then they heard Mr. Bigg's voice at the top of the cellar stairs.

"My workshop is right down here, Mr. Winters," he was saying. "If you liked that painted circus wagon I had on display at my table in the crafts fair, I think you're really going to like what I'm working on downstairs."

After Mr. Bigg spoke, the tiny family heard a loud, friendly voice respond to him. "Mr. Bigg, if what you have in that basement is half as wonderful as that wagon, I should be very interested to see it indeed!" This was followed by a loud, deep laugh.

The Littles heard the sound of footsteps on the cellar stairs. The men were coming down!

"Grab the stuff!" whispered Tom.

Everyone rushed to pick up the rollers and brushes they had been using only a moment before. They quickly threw everything back underneath the paint rag.

With seconds to spare, each tiny person found one small drawer in Mr. Bigg's carpentry cabinet at the back of the workbench. They quickly hid themselves inside of the drawers. Most of them were lucky and got into a drawer with nuts or bolts. Tom found himself lying on an uncomfortable bed of sharp finishing nails.

As the two men reached the middle of the staircase, the Littles watched with horror as Uncle Nick jumped out of his drawer.

He was dressed as usual in one of his major's uniforms. Today, he had worn his casual dress uniform, though, just in case he got paint on himself. He ran like the wind toward the circus. He drew his sword as he ran, and held it over his head.

"Has he gone completely mad?" whispered Mr. Little to Uncle Pete, who was in the drawer next to him. "What in heaven's name is he thinking?"

Uncle Pete was too dumbfounded to speak.

Uncle Nick swooped his sword down through the air. With the point, he picked up a single tiny foam roller that had been left behind on the table. He tossed it off of the tip of his sword, and into a dark corner of the basement.

Mr. Bigg and his friend were almost in the room, and there was no time for Uncle Nick to turn back and hide in the cabinet. Instead, he ran over to a group of painted circus performers and animals. He stood right in the center of the figures. He pointed

his sword at a figurine of a charging lion and stood perfectly still.

When Mr. Bigg walked into the workshop, the tiny people peeked out of the drawers to get a look at Mr. Winters.

Mr. Winters was short and round, with gray hair that came down to his shoulders. He wore glasses, and had a bushy white beard. He was wearing a shiny red satin jacket. On the front were the initials K.W. On the back was a logo with the words "Winter's Wondertoys."

When he saw the circus, he stopped laughing and became very quiet. He began to study it very carefully.

"Mm-hmm," he said to himself. "Mm-hmm, wonderful, really quite amazing..."

He leaned in very closely. His face was inches away from Uncle Nick. Mr. Winters squinted as he looked Uncle Nick over.

"Fabulous!" he said. "The detail in some of these figurines is just brilliant! Very life-like." He chuckled so loudly that his whole belly shook.

He turned to Mr. Bigg. "And you say it's a game, Mr. Bigg?" asked Mr. Winters.

Mr. Bigg explained the rules of the game. Mr. Winters nodded his head, and laughed every so often.

"It's just something I invented for my son, Henry, Mr. Winters," said Mr. Bigg. "It's one of a kind!"

"Not for long, it's not!" His friend laughed. "And please stop calling me Mr. Winters. If we're going to work with each other, call me Klaus."

"Work with each other? That's terrific!" said Mr. Bigg. "Does that mean that you're definitely interested in selling some of my handmade toys as we talked about at the craft fair?"

"Interested in selling—? Oh, that's rich!" Mr. Winters interrupted himself. He laughed so hard his cheeks and nose turned a rosy red. When he stopped laughing, his face became very serious.

"Mr. Bigg, do you have any idea who I

am?" Mr. Winters leaned in toward Mr. Bigg and looked over the tops of his glasses.

"Yes," said Mr. Bigg. "You're Klaus Winters from Winter's Wondertoys."

"Yes, that's true, very true," said his friend. "However, Winter's Wondertoys is just the special handmade toy division of my company. I own a very large toy factory located way, way up north from here. Perhaps you've heard of it? KringleCo Incorporated?"

"Heard of it?" gasped Mr. Bigg. "Of course, I've heard of it! Every home with a kid in it has a KringleCo toy or two! Why, I still set up my KringleCo train set and mess around with it from time to time."

"Mr. Bigg," began Mr. Winters, "may I call you George?"

Mr. Bigg nodded his head.

"George," Mr. Winters went on, "I have a very busy schedule today, so I'm going to get to the point. I want you to join the KringleCo team. You can work right here in your home. Build anything you like, and let me worry about buying the supplies."

"Gee," said Mr. Bigg, "that's awfully nice of you, but I'm afraid I could never make enough toys to support my family, even if I asked a high price for them."

Mr. Winters stared at him for a moment, and then broke into an enormous belly laugh.

"Dear boy," he laughed, "you really don't understand, do you?" He took out a red and white handkerchief and blew his nose with a loud honking sound.

Mr. Bigg shook his head.

"I want you to build prototypes!" said Mr. Winters. "In other words, you create one circus, KringleCo creates thousands of circuses just like it! Maybe more! Oh, of course, we'll have to use different materials than you do, but the toys we build will all stay true to your remarkable vision. I'm prepared to pay you a very handsome salary. And, of course, you'll have a piece of the pie when we patent your inventions. How does that sound?"

"That sounds...wonderful," said Mr. Bigg. He had a very big smile on his face. He leaned on the table. His hand touched the wet paint of the game. He looked at his green finger and frowned.

"Is everything all right, George?" asked Mr. Winters.

Mr. Bigg wiped his finger with a paper towel. "Yes, Klaus," he smiled. "Yes, everything's fine."

"Wonderful!" said Mr. Winters. "I can see it now, George! By next year at this time, lucky kids all over will be waking up to find a KringleCo 'Bigg Top' underneath the Christmas tree!"

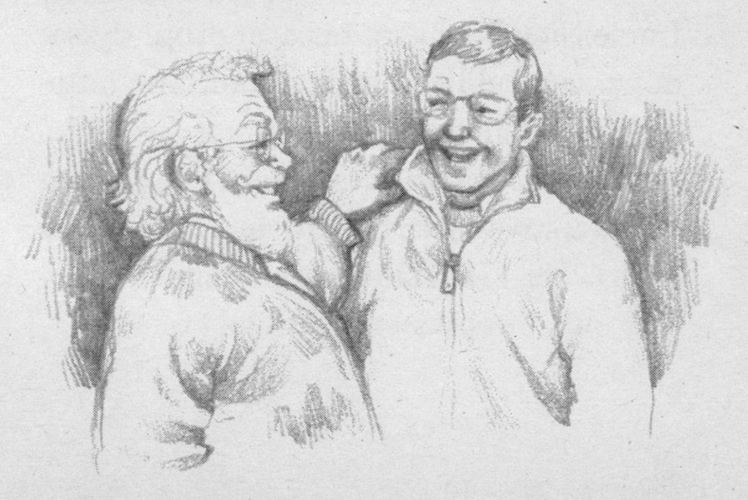

Mr. Winters gave a loud, long laugh. "I'll draw up the contracts right away. Of course, I want you to have your lawyer look them over, just so you're happy with everything, all right?"

"Okay," said Mr. Bigg as the two men shook hands. "Can I offer you anything to eat or drink before you leave?"

"Well," said Mr. Winters, rubbing his belly, "I am very fond of cookies..."

"My wife just baked a batch of chocolate chip cookies," said Mr. Bigg. He gestured to the cellar stairs. "After you, Mr. Winters!"

Mr. Winters laughed. "Klaus, George! Klaus!"

When the two men were safely upstairs, Uncle Nick finally let his arm drop. He sat down and rubbed his shoulder. The Little family all ran over to help him to his feet.

"Ever since I was a little boy, I've wanted to run away to join the circus," Uncle Nick said. "Well, I've finally gotten that little fantasy out of my system! Let's go home!"

11

Later that night, the Littles gathered in their living room to trim their tree. It was a small, tree-shaped piece from the bottom of the Biggs' Christmas tree. Tom and Mr. Little had selected it, cut it, and dragged it home two nights before.

Mrs. Little had taken the box of ornaments out of storage. She and Granny Little were carefully unwrapping them and hanging them on the tree. There were dried cranberries and blueberries, pretty white and pink pebbles, beads, and shiny buttons.

She and Granny wrapped single strands of shiny silver "icicles," which had come from the Biggs' tree, all around their own.

"Where's the star?" asked Mrs. Little.

"Here it is, Wilma," said Granny Little.

She handed it gingerly to Mrs. Little. It was a nice gold star that had come from the top of one of Henry's papers when he was in the first grade.

Mrs. Little looked around. "Where's Lucy?" she asked. "She likes me to pick her up so that she can put the star on top of the tree herself."

"I think I know where she is, Mom," said Tom. "I'll go and get her."

"That's fine, Tom," said his mother. "I'll get things started in the kitchen."

Tom found his sister just where he thought she'd be. She was sitting curled up in one of her favorite spots, a windowsill in the Biggs' attic. She was watching the fresh snow that was gently falling outside.

She could see most of the Biggs' roof as a dusting of snowflakes slowly covered it. The streetlight out front had just come on when Tom sat down next to his sister.

"Isn't it beautiful, Tom?" she said softly. "It's just like that song, a winter wonderland."

Tom nodded.

Lucy spoke again. “Speaking of winter, I liked Mr. Bigg’s new friend. Do you think he’ll come back?”

Tom shrugged. “I don’t know,” he said. “What I do know is that it’s Christmas Eve, and Mom wants you to come downstairs and put the star on the tree. She’s making hot cider for us, too.”

“Hold on a minute,” said Lucy. She picked up a chocolate chip cookie that was lying on the sill next to her. She pushed on a special secret place on the wall, and one of the roof shingles swung open like a trap-door.

Lucy stepped out onto the roof, and walked through the half-inch of new snow over to the chimney. She leaned the cookie carefully against the bricks at the base of the chimney.

Tom watched her as she walked back. She made tiny footprints in the snow. Every so often she stopped for a moment to catch a snowflake in her mouth.

"What the heck were you doing with that cookie?" Tom asked his sister after she had come back inside.

"Just in case he does come back," said Lucy.

"In case who comes back?" said Tom.

"Mr. Winters," whispered Lucy.

"I've got a news flash for you, Lucy," her brother said. "Only tinies walk around on the roof. Big people use the front door, remember?"

"I know," Lucy said quietly. She looked back outside. The snow was slowly covering the cookie. Lucy turned back to her brother.

"Let's go!" she said, dusting snowflakes off of her shoulders. "I want hot cider!"

Tom Little awoke on Christmas morning to a light tapping on his bedroom door. He heard his sister's voice, as she whispered to him. "Tom! Tom! Are you awake yet?"

Tom rubbed the sleep out of his eyes. He turned on the penlight that he kept next to his bed, and pointed it at the strapless wristwatch that hung on his wall. It was seven o'clock in the morning. Tom let his sister into his room.

"I've got our Christmas stockings!" said Lucy. She was very excited.

Mrs. Little had made the two stockings from the thumbs of two old wool mittens. She had embroidered the stockings with patterns of snowflakes.

The children dumped the contents of their stockings out onto Tom's bedspread.

There was a cat's-eye marble, a plastic army man, and a honey-roasted peanut for Tom. Lucy got a new jack, a chocolate-covered raisin, and a purple crayon.

By the time Tom and Lucy ran out to the living room, everyone else was already there.

"Come on, slowpokes!" Grandpa said. "We don't have all day! Let's start opening these presents!"

It was the Littles' custom for each member of the family to receive one special gift, chosen or built especially for them by another member of the family.

Lucy's gift was a beautiful tuffet, made from a small-size cat-food can and a powder puff covered with emerald green silk. She had always wanted a tuffet ever since hearing the rhyme about Miss Muffet. Now she had her own little footstool to sit on while she read.

Mr. Little was as surprised as he could be when he opened up his gift. "Oh, my!" he exclaimed. "A strip of uncanceled History of the American Locomotive stamps! Five different engines—framed and matted, no less!"

He gave Mrs. Little a kiss on the cheek. "Thank you!" he said. "Thank you all!"

The rest of the family went on to open their Christmas presents. Tom got a cool new drum. It was made from the plastic center of a cellophane tape roll, with some fine leather stretched over it. It came with two varnished, hand-carved drumsticks. Grandpa had made them from wooden stick-matches.

Uncle Pete got a hammock fashioned from the string netting that had held a bunch of tangerines.

Granny got a shawl made of light blue satin ribbon trimmed with cotton from an aspirin bottle. She was very proud as she put it around her shoulders and modeled it for the rest of the family.

Baby Betsy, naturally, was more interested in playing with the ribbon on her package than with the new booties Granny had knitted for her.

Uncle Nick's gift was also very special. It was a very old postcard that Cousin Dinky had found in the attic of a house on one of his many adventures.

On the front of it was a photograph of an island with palm trees. On the back was a note from a paratrooper in World War II, to his family back home in Bradford, Pennsylvania. The young soldier wrote that he couldn't wait to come back home after the fighting was over.

Uncle Nick cried a little bit when he was

given his gift, but he pretended that he had gotten something in his eye.

Grandpa Little's gift was just as interesting to the children as it was for him. It was a plastic egg. Inside was a smelly pink goo. The goo could be stretched out like soft rubber. Grandpa would have fun playing with it.

Mrs. Little was the last one to open her gift. Lucy took her mother's hand and pulled her over to the dining table. The whole table was covered by a piece of shiny red and gold Christmas paper.

"What pretty wrapping!" Mrs. Little exclaimed. "I can't guess what this could be."

"Wait 'til you see!" said Lucy. She and Tom took hold of the paper and lifted it up. "Merry Christmas!" they yelled.

"Oh, my!" Mrs. Little gasped.

The table itself was the same one that the family always used. The table setting, on the other hand, was something Mrs. Little had never seen before. And to Mrs. Little, it was like a dream come true.

Mrs. Little had always wanted to eat at a fancy table, like ones she saw sometimes in old movies on the Biggs' television. She often wished they had fancy dishes and glasses and silverware. But they only had plain acorn plates and plastic bottle-cap bowls.

"Do you like it?" Mr. Little asked.

"Like it? I love it!" Mrs. Little said. Her face was glowing. "How did you all do it?" she asked. "Everything is perfect—and just the right size for our family!"

"Oh, we worked on it for a long time," said Mr. Little. "Granny and Grandpa got up early and put everything in place when you were asleep." He pointed to two perfect candles in the center of the table.

"Tom and Lucy melted down leftover bits of Henry Bigg's birthday candles and hand-dipped these new candles themselves. They dipped pieces of dental floss over and over again, until the candles came out just right.

"Grandpa found the plates," he went on. "Can you guess what they are?"

Mrs. Little looked at the glossy red dinner plates. She shook her head no.

"Poker chips!" Grandpa said. "Very old, wooden poker chips. I got them at the same time I got the cards I used to make my antique card table. I always knew they'd be good for something someday!"

Mrs. Little picked up one of the pieces of silverware. "This looks like real silver," she said. "But that's impossible!"

"Impossible?" chimed in Uncle Nick. "Nothing's impossible in Trash City, my dear. Especially if you go to Truck Tiny Town."

"What's that, Uncle Nick?" asked Tom.

"Haven't you heard of Truck Tinies?" asked Uncle Nick. Tom shook his head.

"Truck Tinies pretty much live on garbage trucks," his uncle said. "They travel in and out of the dump underneath the trucks. The truck drivers have no idea that they're there.

"Truck Tinies have seen every inch of the Big Valley, and lots of other places, too. They can pretty much get anything you want, for a price. In this case, I traded one of my swords from Trash City for this silverware. It comes from a long-gone Victorian dollhouse."

"Oh, Uncle Nick," said Mrs. Little. "You love your swords!"

"Pooh, pooh. I have plenty of others," said Uncle Nick.

"Are these place mats real silk?" asked Mrs. Little as she continued to walk around the table.

"Yep," said Granny Little. "They're dress swatches from the bridesmaids' outfits when Mrs. Bigg's sister got married. That's why each one is a different color."

"The tablecloth and drinking glasses are borrowed from the attic, and I'm afraid they'll have to go back in a while," said Mr. Little. "Mrs. Bigg might miss her great grandmother's antique lace handkerchief and china thimble collection."

Mrs. Little picked up one of the thimbles. Each one was white with a different scene painted in blue. The artwork was fancy and old-fashioned. A thin, silver band ran around the top of each thimble.

Mrs. Little looked around at the smiling faces of her family.

"Merry Christmas!" they all said.

Mrs. Little laughed. "Well, Merry Christmas to all of you, too!" she said. "Thank you all so much. Never in a million years did I expect anything as special as this."

She smiled as she wiped a tiny tear from the corner of her eye. She looked over the beautiful table settings once again. "Oh, I just thought of something: What's for dinner?"

"Roast duck with all the trimmings!" said Uncle Pete.

"When do we eat?" asked Lucy. "I'm starving!"

"Just as soon as the Biggs are done with their roast duck dinner," said Granny.

Lucy sighed. "Some things never change," she said.

After their Christmas dinner, the Littles sat around their living room enjoying one another's company. They were sipping spiced apple cider from their china thimble glasses.

Grandpa, Tom, and Lucy were playing with Grandpa's present. They were rolling the pink goo flat on pictures of people in an old newspaper they'd found. When they peeled it off, the picture from the paper was printed on the goo. Then they laughed as they stretched the pictures out, giving the people very funny faces and expressions.

"Let's see if we can get some news," said Uncle Nick. He stood up and put his finger to his lips.

The Littles grew silent as he pulled the cork out of the wall. Now they could hear what was going on in the Biggs' living room.

"I think that was the best duck I've ever had," Mr. Bigg was saying.

"Henry!" They heard Mrs. Bigg call out. "Close the front door! You're letting out all the heat!" She spoke more quietly to her husband. "Do you know that this is the first time all day that he's been away from his circus? I don't know which one of my boys loves that game more, Henry or you, George!"

The Littles heard the front door close, and heard Henry's footsteps and Callie's dog tags as the two of them ran into the living room.

"Wow!" said Henry. "There must be two feet of snow out there! And it's still coming down!"

"Too bad we don't have a sleigh," Mrs. Bigg said. "We could go for a sleigh ride!"

Then she began to sing: "Jingle bells, jingle bells, jingle all the way..."

The Little family listened as Henry and Mr. Bigg joined in. The three of them grew louder and louder with each verse. Suddenly, Lucy began to sing along!

At first, her family was shocked that she would dare to sing out loud with the Bigg family. But then they realized that the Biggs were singing so loudly they couldn't tell that Lucy had joined them.

One by one, each member of the tiny family began to sing "Jingle Bells." Soon, every person in the house, big or small, was singing along.

When the song was over, everything somehow felt more like Christmas than it had only a moment before. On the other side of the wall, they could hear Mr. Bigg talking again.

"This year has been a very special Christmas," he was saying to his family. "For a while there, I was really worried that things weren't going to work out for us."

"But they did," said Mrs. Bigg.

"They sure did," said her husband. "With help from the two of you, and Mr. Winters, and..."

"And?" asked his wife.

"And who knows? Help seems to come to you when you need it the most," said Mr. Bigg. "Someone sure was on my side this time, and I'm thankful for that."

Inside the Littles' living room, Lucy turned to her family. "Do you think he means us?" she whispered.

Her father shook his head. "No. Shhhh!" he whispered.

"George?" said Mrs. Bigg. "You have such a good singing voice. Sing that Christmas song I love. You know the one I mean?"

The Littles listened as George Bigg began to sing. His voice was strong and clear as he started the song, "Have Yourself a Merry Little Christmas."

Lucy had never heard the song before. "See? See?" she bounced up and down on the sofa as she whispered excitedly. "Have yourself a merry *Little* Christmas! He's singing just for us! I know it!"

As he went on singing, Lucy put her head right next to the cork hole. There was just a thin layer of wallpaper between her and the Biggs. She whispered very softly.

"Merry Christmas, Mr. Bigg. Merry Christmas, Mrs. Bigg, Henry, Hildy, and Callie." She turned back to her family and whispered a little bit louder: "Merry Christmas, everyone!"

That night, as it snowed and snowed outside, the Bigg family continued to sing one great old Christmas carol after another. And the Littles helped them out with every single one.